AF243721

Other works by the author

Ticket to Ride

Hatred is the key

We're gonna be famous

Graham Sclater

Tabitha

Graham Sclater

Published in 2009 by Tabitha Books

Copyright © 2009 Graham Sclater

First Edition

The author asserts the moral right under the Copyright, Design
and Patents Act 1988 to be identified as the author of this work.

All the characters in this publication are fictitious and any
resemblance to real persons, living or dead is purely coincidental.

All Rights reserved.

No part of this publication may be reproduced, stored in a
retrieval system, or transmitted, in any form or by any means without
the prior written consent of the author, nor be otherwise circulated in
any form of binding or cover other than that in which it is published
and without a similar condition being imposed on the subsequent
purchaser.

Tabitha Books is a Division of Tabitha Music Limited
Exeter EX2 9DJ

Author Graham Sclater is based in Devon where he works as a music publisher and songwriter. He has lived and worked as a musician for many years playing and recording all over the world and working with many successful artists. He recently began writing and his first novel "Ticket to Ride" was published by Flame Books. He is currently working on a number of television series and screenplays.

Graham Sclater

Cover design and artwork by Feddy

With thanks to Feddy for the fabulous artwork, Denise for editing my work, Julie Khan for her inspiration, Girls Aloud and the Sugababes for their great music, the Corrs for their wonderful music while I was writing and all at Tabitha Music.

Graham Sclater

Track one - Girls

Track two - Angels with dirty faces

Track three - I say a prayer for you

Track four - Push the button

Track five - Some kind of miracle

Track six - Never gonna dance again

Track seven - Life got cold

Track eight - Caught in a moment

Track nine - The Promise

Track ten - Lush life

'I know I'll be a star one day, Hannah,' said Abi as she smiled at her big sister.

'I believe you… so will I,' said Hannah as she grinned and nodded.

Graham Sclater

We're gonna be famous

'Everyone has a dream but how many realise it?'

We're gonna be famous

Girls

'Come on Abi. Turn off that music or you're going to be late for school… again,' pleaded Mr Thomas. He shook his head at his youngest daughter in disbelief as he tried desperately to tidy the flat before attending to the gruelling cleaning task downstairs in the ground floor bar and restaurant.

Abi Thomas, aged 8, was a pretty girl, her unbrushed long blonde curly hair fell onto her narrow shoulders. Her pale blue school blouse hung unevenly outside of her grey pleated skirt.

The blouse buttons were once again done up lopsided, making it look as though she was wearing a blouse two sizes too small for her.

Abi didn't like school, preferring to play her music and dance which, every morning without fail, left her with little or no time to get dressed properly.

'Yes, come on Abi, we're always late,' shrieked Hannah, Abi's ten year old sister.

'Why do I always get detention because of you?' she shouted.

Hannah took pride in her appearance always ensuring that her dark brown hair was immaculate and that her school uniform was always ironed. She wasn't as pretty as Abi but was very grown up for her age and her confidence and tidiness of appearance made her stand out amongst the other girls in her class.

Abi and Hannah were both obsessed with pop music, much to the detriment of their homework, spending every spare minute singing along with their favourite pop songs and dancing along with the video clips on MTV. And, even when they finally went to bed they would stay awake hiding under the covers listening, with headphones, to the local radio station.

The school bus sounded its horn outside the Hare and Hounds, a quaint pub on the outskirts of Littlehampstead, a small picture postcard village in the middle of the Somerset countryside.

Still eating their toast, Abi and Hannah rushed down the narrow winding staircase and out through the darkened bar.

Their father called after them, 'Don't forget it's karaoke tonight, so don't be late home. It's going to be very busy this evening and you'll need to have your tea early so that I can get things ready.'

The sisters were used to fending for themselves, with Hannah usually cooking the tea for herself, Abi, their mother, and even occasionally for her father. They didn't reply, and he stood at the top of the stairs shaking his head and talking to himself.

'Girls, who'd have 'em?' he said.

He thought for a moment before smiling and then continued, 'I wouldn't be without 'em though.'

They didn't hear him because they were gone, running out into the warm summer sunshine and onto the dark green and white striped school bus waiting at the edge of the car park.

'Morning girls,' said George Simpson, the school bus driver. As well as being a regular at the Hare and Hounds, his wife taught modern dance, the most popular after school activity. He knew them and their father well and, because he was aware that their mother was sick, he always waited longer than he should, and made allowances for them to at least try to eat some of their breakfast before rushing out to catch the bus.

'Morning George,' replied Abi and Hannah

both smiling at him, before excitedly greeting their friends and running down to the back of the bus and both squeezing into the only empty seat with their best friend Rosie. There was an air of great excitement on the school bus today because there were only three days left at school before the start of the long summer holiday, the following Tuesday.

When Rosie Ferndale, who was the same age as Hannah, moved to the area with her parents and elder brother, Josh, aged 20, she joined the modern dance class and soon became close friends with Abi and Hannah. The three of them would often sneak into the pub lounge on Saturday mornings, before it opened, to sing along with their favourite songs, using the karaoke equipment prior to the owner taking it away to another club or pub.

Rosie's father was an executive in the music business in London, and her mother a successful magazine publisher. Because both parents often worked away during the week, Nana Ferndale, their father's mother, had chosen to move into the Granny flat adjoining the house from where she could look after Rosie and keep an eye on Josh.

As Mr Thomas, looking tired and drawn, hurriedly tidied the girls' rooms, his wife Emily woke up and called out to him from the bedroom at the end of the landing. 'Bobby,' her voice was weak and sounded very tired.

'Yes love, I'm coming,' he replied, as he walked along the landing towards the open door of the bedroom where his wife lay in bed.

He entered the darkened room, walked across to the window and pulled open the curtains, allowing the bright sunlight to rush in and flood the dismal and depressing room.

'How do you feel today?' he asked as he leant over and kissed her on the forehead.

'Not too bad,' she lied as she fidgeted and

tried to get comfortable. 'What a lovely sunny morning, I wish I could get up to see it,' she said.

'You will.' He smiled. 'I bet you'll be up enjoying the summer soon.'

He knew that her health had deteriorated over the last few weeks and he awaited Doctor Hughes' daily visits with trepidation.

Even before Emily had had time to finish her meagre breakfast, Doctor Hughes, a bespectacled, overweight, grey haired man, let himself in, and climbed the staircase to his patient's room. After climbing so many stairs he sat down on the chair beside the bed and caught his breath before continuing. He gave her a thorough check up, took her temperature and pulse, then listened to her chest before shining a torch into her eyes. He methodically put his stethoscope back into its allotted space in one of the many pockets in his old worn black leather bag, and cleared his throat before speaking.

'I'm not too happy with your condition, Mrs

Thomas.' He paused. 'I feel that we should get you into hospital and carry out some tests. I'll arrange for an ambulance,' he said.

She smiled gratefully at the Doctor and then at her husband, who reached out, held her hand and pressed it reassuringly.

Later that afternoon, just as the school bus pulled up outside the Hare and Hounds, an ambulance drove into the car park. Abi and Hannah were busy singing with Rosie and the rest of their school friends. They all tried desperately to remember the steps that they had been rehearsing for the last hour in the modern dance and singing class, organized by Mrs Simpson, their music teacher.

When the sisters saw the ambulance, they jumped off the bus and without saying goodbye to their friends, ran towards the side door that led up to their flat above the pub.

George shouted after them. 'See you on Monday girls.'

They were so worried that they didn't hear him.

As the school bus pulled away everyone on board stood up and stared out of the windows at the ambulance. They all talked excitedly, imagining all sorts of wild and weird thoughts as to why it was there and what had happened.

Angels with dirty faces

Abi and Hannah rushed up the narrow stairs, threw their school bags into the lounge then ran down the corridor to their mother's bedroom. Although this had happened many times before they were still shocked as they stood and watched the paramedics lift their mother onto the stretcher and then negotiate their way down the dark staircase and out into the car park.

The bright afternoon sunshine temporarily blinded their mother and she tried desperately to turn her head away. Her husband rushed across to her and shielded her eyes from the sun.

The girls stood watching helplessly as the paramedics lifted their mother into the back of the ambulance, closed the doors and gently drove away.

Mr Thomas started the engine and they all followed in the old and rusty estate car.

Even their father was subdued as he drove through the narrow country lanes keeping as close to the ambulance as he dared without risking an accident. He made a number of attempts to reassure Abi and Hannah but as soon as he realised that his efforts were useless they made the remainder of the short journey to Summerfield Hospital in total silence.

Within fifteen minutes, the ambulance and their car raced through the gates and into the hospital car park. Mr Thomas parked the car and tried to pull on the handbrake but it took three attempts before it finally clicked on the ratchet.

Abi and Hannah jumped out of the car and

rushed across to the entrance, dodging other cars, taxis and speeding ambulances with flashing blue lights, while their father struggled impatiently to lock the doors.

The girls struggled to catch their breath and stood on the wide pavement at the entrance. They were greeted by a pretty young nurse who waited with them until their father was able to join them. She led them along what seemed like mile upon mile of identical pale yellow painted corridors, into the lift and up to a family waiting room on the third floor.

The three of them waited in silence and as the realization of the seriousness gradually took over, the two sisters became more and more upset. When Abi noticed that her father had tears in his eyes she began to sob uncontrollably.

Hannah, trying hard to hold back her own tears, grabbed at her younger sister, 'Come on Abi, let's get a drink,' she said.

Mr Thomas put his hand in his pocket and,

without looking up, handed Hannah a handful of coins. He turned and stood, blindly staring out of the window, as he silently feared what the doctors might tell him.

Abi and Hannah soon returned and sat quietly in the corner, sipping the hot drinks, as they both impatiently thumbed through the out of date and torn magazines.

When the door handle turned they all looked up towards the door and waited for it to open. Doctor Fitzsimmons, the specialist, wearing an ill-fitting white coat, entered the waiting room. 'Could I talk to you please?'

He looked at Mr Thomas and then at the girls.

'Of course,' replied their father. He turned to face the doctor and gave a half smile.

Doctor Fitzsimmons stood upright and thrust his hands deep in to his white coat pockets while his eyes darted impatiently between the girls and their father, sending a silent message to Mr Thomas. The doctor screwed up his face, then opened his eyes wide before repeating the request several times until Mr Thomas eventually understood.

Realising that the doctor wanted to talk to him in private, he whispered to the girls. 'Go on Hannah, take Abi and get yourselves another drinking chocolate from the machine.'

Although they were unwilling to leave their father they realised that the doctor would not speak to him while they were in the room.

'I'm fed up with this,' moaned Abi. 'Can't we get something to eat?' she said.

Reluctantly, they both shuffled out of the room and Dr Fitzsimmons motioned to Mr Taylor to sit down on the brightly flowered settee. He smiled and sat down opposite him in a matching armchair.

'I'm afraid the news isn't good,' he said taking a deep breath. 'Mrs Thomas has a very rare blood condition. Unfortunately, it's so rare that we are unable to treat it in this country.' He could see the effect that the bad news was having on Mr Thomas and continued in a much softer but more positive voice. 'That doesn't mean that help isn't available,' he said reassuringly.

Mr Thomas stopped and looked at him, tense and impatient, as he waited to hear some good news.

Doctor Fitzsimmons smiled briefly, 'I don't want to raise your hopes too high but....'

Mr Thomas sank back in his chair, frustrated that he was to be disappointed yet again. 'There is a radical specialist in California who could treat your wife... but...,' he paused, 'it will be very expensive. We can assist with some of the costs but not all of them....'

At that moment Abi and Hannah burst into the room, each carrying a plastic cup of hot drinking chocolate and a packet of crisps. They both sensed that the news was not good but Abi, unable to contain her feelings any longer, blurted out impulsively. 'She's going to die... isn't she?'

'Come on Abs, sit down,' pleaded her father. He stood up, put his arms around his two daughters, and slowly explained the situation to them.

'Surely there's something we can do?' screamed Hannah.

'Yes there is,' interrupted the doctor. 'But, as I explained to your father, it will cost a great deal of money. We can help with some of the costs but you will need much more, and unfortunately that sort of money isn't available from the Health Service.'

'Doctor, do you have any idea how much we will need?' asked Mr Thomas.

The Doctor scratched his head and thought for a few seconds as he added up the costs in mid-air on an imaginary calculator. He screwed up his face and took another deep breath. 'Well….' He tilted his head to one side, took a deep breath and continued. 'I suppose… somewhere in the region of ten thousand pounds.'

The girls looked at each other wide eyed as he continued. 'And, of course you will need the air fare,' he said.

Abi and Hannah, now stunned and speechless, squeezed onto the settee beside their father. He put his arms around them and stroked their shoulders lovingly. They sat staring at the floor and, as the seriousness of their mother's illness gradually began to sink in, they both tried frantically to remember every word that Doctor Fitzsimmons had said to them.

I say a prayer for you

As they all travelled home from the hospital, their father tried to reassure them.

'Come on girls, something will turn up, it always does. We will get the money somehow.' He lied to them because he was as worried as they were, but he was not prepared to tell them or let them see his concern.

Abi decided to sleep in the spare bed in Hannah's room that night and, after cleaning their teeth and saying a prayer for their mother, their father kissed them goodnight and turned out the light.

Subconsciously, their minds raced as they listened to the transistor radio while at the same time tried to think of ways that they could raise the money.

In the darkness Abi started to feel frightened. 'Hannah… do you think that Mum is going to die?' she asked as she felt the tears running down her cheeks onto the soft pink cotton pillow.

'I don't know Abs. She can't. Who's going to look after us?' replied her sister.

Hannah also started to cry but she turned her head away and pushed her face into the pillow so that Abi couldn't see her. 'I wish we could help Mum,' sobbed Hannah. 'I wish I'd never spent any of my pocket money. If I'd saved it then I could have given it to Doctor Fitzsimmons for Mum's treatment so that she could get better.'

'We could clean cars in the car park at the weekend,' suggested Abi. 'And… Hannah,' she waited for an idea. 'And you could get a paper round,' she suggested excitedly.

'It's a good idea Abi but it will take us years,' sighed Hannah, feeling frustrated at the hopeless situation.

The radio played to itself but something suddenly attracted Hannah's attention. 'Hold on Abi. Did you hear that?' she shouted excitedly.

'Yes listeners that's right. Seven thousand pounds could be yours. All you have to do is………'

The voice of the DJ on the local radio station became inaudible as Abi interrupted. 'Imagine what we could do if we had all that,' she said, hardly able to hold back her enthusiasm.

'Be quiet. Just listen will you!' screamed Hannah as she pressed her hands across Abi's mouth.

The DJ faded out the music and then continued. *'Do you think you could write a song? That's all you have to do. And you could be on your way to fame and fortune like Girls Aloud and*

Britney. The closing date is next Monday, so get your entries in now.'

'God, Abi! That could be us! We could do that,' shrieked Hannah excitedly.

Abi could feel Hannah's excitement rubbing off on her. 'Then we could give Dad the money to take Mum to America. And she would get better… and we'd be famous,' she gushed.

She looked up at the huge posters of their favourite pop stars covering every square inch of her bedroom wall, and dreamed. Perhaps they could be as famous as their idols already were.

Hannah stood on her bed getting more excited as the idea and opportunity took her over. 'Don't just lie there Abi, get a pen and paper. We could write a rap….'

'And a dance,' interrupted Abi.

She jumped off her bed and started to pose, flicking one hand through her hair and holding her hairbrush with the other, before dancing around the bedroom pretending that the hairbrush was a microphone.

They spent the next few hours writing and then crossing out line after line of words until they felt that they had the beginnings of a song.

The next day was Saturday and for once they were awake before their father. They put on their dressing gowns and slippers, and sneaked downstairs into the bar where the karaoke equipment was still set up from the previous night. They argued over the words until they'd thought of a tune.

The words slowly began to fit the music and they recorded the song using the karaoke machine. When they were satisfied with their efforts they crept back upstairs for an early breakfast, then back to bed to catch up on the sleep they'd missed the night before.

They didn't sleep for long and within an hour they were sitting at the table eating their second breakfast of the morning. As they ate their cereal they found it hard to control the excitement of writing and recording their first song and they desperately wanted to play it to someone.

They were interrupted by the sound of a vehicle driving across the car park gravel. Abi rushed to the window, pulled back the curtains, climbed onto a chair and saw the ambulance doors open and the paramedics carefully lifting their mother out.

'Its Mum, they've brought her home. Do you think she's better?' shrieked Abi.

Their father joined them at the window. 'Well come on. Let's go down and welcome your mother home,' he said.

Mrs Thomas was soon back in her bed and she sat patiently waiting for her breakfast while her husband tried to tell her what Doctor Fitzsimmons had told him.

She smiled as she spoke, 'Well maybe he was wrong. They're not always right you know… I tell you what, why don't we get a second opinion?' she said.

Bobby smiled back at her and nodded. 'Alright, that's a good idea. He thought for a moment and continued. 'Why not?' he replied.

The opportunity for Abi and Hannah to play their song to someone came a few minutes later when the telephone rang. Because Rosie's parents were away for the day, she invited Abi and Hannah to her house for tea.

The sisters found it hard to get the song out of their heads and while they showered and prepared their mother's breakfast, they repeatedly sang the song over and over.

'I'm sure we can win,' hummed Abi as she buttered the toast.

'Maybe,' replied Hannah, as she tried to remember the steps that she had taught Abi.

'If we win, do you think that we will get to be on MTV?' asked Abi.

''Course we will,' replied Hannah, trying to humour her sister.

Hannah carried the tray while Abi followed

close behind with the morning paper. Mrs Thomas looked forward to the paper and she always read it from end to end, including the sports pages.

'What are you two so happy about? You both seem unusually pleased with yourselves this morning?' asked their mother, smiling as she sat up in bed and pressed down the duvet to form a flat surface for the tray.

Abi started to tell her mother about their song but Hannah dug her elbow hard into Abi's ribs.

'We break up from school next week,' gushed Hannah as she interrupted her sister.

Abi turned and was about to shout at her when Hannah whispered into her ear, 'It's a secret,' she said.

Abi nodded and gave a knowing smile and began to grin from ear to ear.

Hannah continued to answer her mother's question, 'and then…,' she put her finger into her mouth and thought.

'…and then we have a lovely long holiday,'

blurted out Abi, realising that she had nearly given the game away.

Push the button

Relieved that they had not given away their secret they settled down and took it in turns to read the paper to their mother while she ate her breakfast. As soon as she finished clearing her plate and drinking all her tea Hannah picked up the tray, washed the dishes, and they both rushed out into the back yard to leave their mother in peace to rest and re-read the paper.

While Abi collected up the empty plastic beer crates, Hannah struggled with the old scaffold boards left behind by the builders. They built a makeshift stage against the cellar wall and although it was a bit rickety, they were at last able to practise miming to the tape recording and polish up the dance routine until they were confident they could perform it to Rosie without making too many mistakes.

Neither of them felt hungry, they were both much too excited. They rushed their lunch and, without saying goodbye to their mother or father, left the Hare and Hounds.

As they cycled along the country lane they sang the song at the top of their voices, both of them getting more and more excited as they got nearer to Rosie's house.

Rosie sat and listened as the music played loudly out of her father's high tech music system and watched Abi and Hannah perform the dance that they had created to go with it.

Rosie loved it.

'That's fantastic. Did you really write it?' she asked.

''Course we did,' replied Hannah and Abi

simultaneously.

'Can I dance with you if you win?' asked Rosie.

'Yeah, of course, it's more fun with three of us anyway,' replied Abi.

Their fun was short lived and, following numerous frantic telephone calls to their school friends, their father finally found them at Rosie's and asked Nana Ferndale to tell them to return home immediately.

Worried about what their father would say, they peddled the short distance home in silence, and, after putting their bikes in the shed they nervously climbed the stairs.

Their father was waiting for them in the lounge and fired off at them without taking a breath. 'What do you think you're doing? Me and your mother have been worried stiff. It's the last thing she needs. Don't you realise how poorly she is? It's this sort of selfish attitude that makes… Well, both of you get to your rooms now… and…. none of that music. This is a punishment!' His face said it all and the girls knew it was totally pointless to argue with him.

Some kind of miracle

The following morning Hannah telephoned the radio station for their address and, after borrowing an envelope and stamp from her father, started to write the letter. 'Abi can you get me the cassette,' she asked. 'We need to post it today or we'll miss the closing date.'

Abi looked at her strangely. 'I haven't got it. I thought you were looking after it,' she said.

Hannah's face suddenly changed from happy to angry. 'Come on Abigail.' She always called her by her full name when she was angry. 'Give me the tape, the sooner we post it the better,' she said impatiently tapping the pen on the table.

'I told you, I haven't got the lousy tape,'

pleaded Abi.

They searched the flat to no avail and as a last resort they pulled the cushions off of the settee and armchairs, throwing them across the room, and thrusting their tiny hands down every crevice.

When Abi found several coins and an old earring that her mother had lost the Christmas before last, she shrieked with excitement.

'Look Hannah, I've found some money,' Hannah walked across the room and took the coins from her and carefully examined them. 'These are worthless, with the exception of that fifty pence piece the rest are foreign coins.' Their father always gave them the useless coins that he'd been given by customers who'd been abroad on holiday.

But Abi was still positive and raised her voice, 'They might be worth something, can't we check?' she asked in desperation.

'Perhaps a pound, but only if we can exchange them,' said Hannah. And, as she handed them back to Abi, she slowly shook her head. 'This is a total waste of time. It can't be here or we would have found it by now.'

Abi suddenly had a brainwave and her face lit up. 'Hold on, maybe Dad's got it.'

They rushed down the stairs into the crowded bar and tried to attract their father's attention.

Finally, he noticed them. 'I am extremely busy girls. What is it you want?' he asked, clearly annoyed.

Hannah took charge. 'Dad, have you seen a cassette in the flat?' she asked.

'Yes Dad,' interrupted Abi. 'A cassette tape… it is very important,' she said.

Their father tried to think but he was more concerned about the customers queuing all along the bar and mumbling to each other as they waited impatiently to be served. 'Cassette? No,' he said. 'I've got absolutely no idea what you're talking about.' He turned back to his customers. 'Yes Harry, the usual?' he asked.

He smiled and, oblivious to Abi and Hannah standing behind him, he pulled two pints of bitter.

Their jaws dropped with disappointment and frustration and realising that he could not help them, he turned away.

'Come on Hannah let's go back upstairs and have a look in our bedrooms,' whispered Abi.

'Oh, what's the point? I know we're only wasting our time,' replied Hannah.

They searched every inch of the flat for the second time, turning out cassettes and CD's that they'd forgotten they owned. And all the while, they became more and more upset.

They put on a video of Britney and sat on the settee watching the screen, but on this occasion they had no absolutely interest in it at all. Instead they both tried desperately to remember where the cassette might be.

'Let's think. When was the last time we had it?' asked Hannah.

They half closed their eyes and stared blindly

across the room deep in thought.

'Well, we played it to Rosie yesterday afternoon…,' said Abi.

'Then we had tea,' continued Hannah.

'Then Dad phoned us,' shrieked Abi.

'Yes, that's right,' remembered Hannah excitedly. 'So we must have left it at Rosie's house….'

Abi gave a great sigh of relief.

Hannah always blamed her for anything that went wrong or something she hadn't done. She jumped up, ran out to the hall, picked up the telephone and called Rosie.

The phone rang for several minutes before Nana Ferndale answered. 'Hello, who is it?'

'It's Hannah Thomas,' she blurted out.

'Who?' asked Nana Ferndale.

Hannah slowly spelt her name, 'H…A…N…N…A…H. Could I speak to Rosie please?' she asked, her desperation clearly audible in her high pitched voice.

'I'm sorry they've gone on holiday,' she paused as she checked the dates. 'Back in four weeks,' she said. And with that she replaced the receiver.

Hannah stood holding the telephone until Abi lost her patience. 'Well, has she got it?' she asked.

'She's gone on holiday,' said Hannah in almost a whisper.

'What? shouted Abi.

'For… *four weeks*!' sighed Hannah screwing up her face as she shook her head slowly, then faster as the bad news began to sink in.

'Well come on, let's cycle over and see if we can find it,' shouted Abi.

They raced down the lane until they reached Rosie's large house, rang the doorbell, and waited… and waited. Nana Ferndale was very deaf and didn't hear them, so they walked around to the rear of the house.

Josh, wearing his designer sunglasses and designer tee-shirt and shorts, lay on a sun lounger in the garden enjoying the warm summer sunshine. Although he wore large headphones, the music of Oasis also pumped out from his ghetto blaster, making him oblivious to everything and everyone around him.

Nana Ferndale was fast asleep in a deckchair, enjoying the peace, under a large bright yellow and red umbrella, while Harriet, Rosie's Yorkshire terrier, sat on her lap enjoying the regained luxury that Rosie used to afford her when she first adopted her from Battersea Dogs Home in London.

Abi and Hannah dropped their bikes, ran over and gently shook Nana Ferndale until she woke up. She jumped with surprise, causing Harriet to squeal as she fell awkwardly onto the grass. Nana Ferndale took a few moments to focus her tired eyes before recognising Abi and Hannah standing in front of her. 'What are you doing here?' she asked.

They were so excited that they both spluttered

and spoke at the same time. 'We need to speak to Rosie,' they said.

'I'm sorry dearies, please speak one at a time or I can't hear you either of you.' She fumbled as she adjusted her hearing aid. 'Now, what is it you want?'

Hannah pushed Abi to one side, 'We need to talk to Rosie,' she said.

Nana Ferndale tried to speak but Hannah interrupted her and continued. 'We know that she's gone on holiday but we still need to talk to her. Do you have the telephone number where she's staying?' she asked.

Nana Ferndale appeared very confused and took a while to gather her thoughts. 'Now let me see....'

The two girls stood waiting on her every word.

'I know that they were going to France,' she said.

'Mm... ye...eas,' mumbled Hannah expectantly. 'Go on.'

'Then, they're going to Italy and back through Spain to catch the ferry from Santander to Plymouth.' She was pleased with herself as she remembered their itinerary.

'That's great. But do you have a telephone number for any of the places that she's visiting?' asked Hannah, nodding her head.

'Oh no dear, of course not, they like to travel in peace. No interruptions from work you know. They work very hard and need a break from all that.'

Abi spoke up. 'But you must be able to contact them if there was an emergency?'

'Well, do you know I never thought of that,' said Nana Ferndale.

She sat thinking for a few seconds and then, pleased with herself, smiled and continued. 'Maybe they'll telephone me at some point.' She smiled broadly. 'If they do, I'll tell them that you want to speak to Rosie.'

'It will be too late by then. Are you really sure

you don't have a number for her?' asked Hannah, making one final attempt at jogging Nana Ferndale's memory.

'Or a mobile?' asked Abi.

'No dearies… they didn't want any interruptions… this is their holiday you know,' she scolded. 'They want some peace and time to relax.'

Josh turned over on his sun lounger and moaned at the intrusion of his privacy by the young girls. One girl in the house was bad enough and he was glad to be rid of his younger sister for a few weeks. But no sooner had she gone, the very next day two more arrived uninvited.

Abi and Hannah turned and walked slowly back to their bikes and didn't hear Nana Ferndale offer them a glass of cool orange juice and a biscuit. They had other things on their minds.

'Well that's it then,' said Hannah as they cycled along the lane.

'Can't we record it again?' suggested Abi

excitedly.

'Don't you think that I haven't already thought of that?' she cussed. 'You must think I'm stupid. Of course I have, but the karaoke equipment won't be back until next weekend.'

'Oh well, that's it then,' shrugged Abi. 'There's no way that we will be able to help Mum now is there?'

Never gonna dance again

They cycled as fast as they could and Abi tried desperately to keep up with Hannah who always won every race.

They rushed back to the pub and tried to explain the situation to their father but he was much too preoccupied with running the pub and looking after their mother. He often worked well into the night when the pub closed, washing and ironing the girls' clothes and cleaning the flat before finally going to bed.

Abi and Hannah spent much of the holiday looking after their mother, whose health was gradually deteriorating further, with her often spending several days at a time in bed.

The only relief was listening to their CD's or the radio.

After yet another emergency visit, Doctor Hughes told them that their mother needed the specialist treatment urgently. His last words caused the girls even greater upset. 'Your mother is very ill and she needs to rest. She also needs as much peace and quiet as she can get.'

He looked at Mr Thomas and across to Hannah and Abi. With a stern look on his face, he continued. 'I would suggest that you restrict any noise, such as music or television, as much as possible,' he said as he closed his bag.

Hannah and Abi were devastated but, not wishing to upset their mother, agreed that they wouldn't play any music upstairs until she was better.

For the next few weeks the flat above the pub was like a morgue, the silence was terrible, but it worked, and for a while their mother's health seemed to improve.

Emily liked having the girls around to talk to her and sometimes the three of them played Scrabble. She even made it to the garden on a few warm afternoons, but on the fourth week the peace was broken.

Abi and Hannah were washing their hair ready for the evening's karaoke when their father, shouting to them from the landing, interrupted their fun.

'Quick Hannah, phone an ambulance. Mum's had a relapse,' he shouted.

In the hospital, they stood around the bed and watched as their mother was connected to numerous drips, tubes and machines, oblivious to the drama going on around her.

Doctor Fitzsimmons turned and, unable to hide his concern, he spoke to the three of them in a soft voice. 'I'm sorry but there is little more that we can do for your mother. We can of course stabilise her condition but she desperately needs the specialist treatment that I mentioned to you the last time you were here.'

'Thank you doctor,' replied Mr Thomas, nodding slowly, confirming his understanding of the seriousness of the situation.

Abi and Hannah walked back into the ward and sat with their mother for a few minutes until the nurse asked them to leave.

They took it in turns to kiss their mother before they left the hospital and waited in the car park for their father.

The journey back home was very depressing their father turned on the radio to help take their mind off their mother's illness.

The DJ faded the latest single by Westlife and began to speak excitedly. '*Well listeners, at last I can tell you the name of the winner of our songwriting competition, and play you their song.*'

The music started, and after a few seconds Hannah screamed. 'That's our song.'

'I can't believe it,' shouted Abi excitedly.

'Come on girls, of course it is,' joked their father sarcastically.

'It is our song,' insisted Hannah as she looked across at her father.

'It's true dad, we did write it, but we lost the tape,' said Abi almost out of breath.

'Well if you did, and I'm not saying whether you did or not. How did it get on the radio?' he asked.

Before they could answer, the DJ faded out the music. *'What a great song.'* He faded up the chorus of the song and then down again, *'The successful winner of our songwriting competition is….'*

'How did that happen?' screamed Hannah.

'We lost the tape that's why,' spluttered Abi.

'Just listen, will you,' interrupted Hannah.

Mr Thomas braked hard and pulled into a lay by, and they all sat waiting with baited breath. The DJ teased the listeners. *'Winning the first prize of seven thousand pounds it's…,'* there was silence until he faded up the music again, *'It's…Josh Ferndale of Littlehampstead.'*

'What?' shouted Hannah?

'How did he?' screamed the two girls.

'That's not fair!' shouted Abi.

'The cheat!' screamed Hannah.

'Come on kids, give him credit. That's a good song. How could you write something as good as that? It sounded really professional.' He started the car and drove out of the lay by.

'But we did!' insisted Abi and Hannah, beginning to lose their voices with anger.

Josh was sitting in the studio and after thanking the DJ. He told him that he was going to use the money to fund his year long College trip to Africa. Something he thought he would not be able to do until he won the competition.

It angered Abi and Hannah and they continued to shout insults at the radio.

'The creep!' screamed Hannah.

'That's enough now girls,' pleaded their father. 'What would your mother think if she could hear you now?' he said.

Their father drove into the pub car park, locked the car, and left them to start his work in the bar. They shuffled up the stairs and into Hannah's room in silence, too upset to speak or to eat anything.

They both lay on Hannah's bed staring at the huge posters as they tried to think.

'If we can prove that Josh didn't write that song we will have almost enough money for Mum's treatment,' Abi suggested.

'How do you think we can do that?' snapped Hannah.

'I don't know. I really don't,' mumbled Abi.

She cried herself to sleep while Hannah laid thinking of what might have been, and cursing Josh.

Resigned to their hopelessness, Abi and Hannah

spent the rest of their holiday counting the days and waiting for Rosie to return, knowing that she was the only person who could prove that they did write the song.

When she returned from holiday, Hannah telephoned her on numerous occasions, but every time she rang, Josh answered, assuring her that he would pass on her message.

'She's avoiding us,' said Abi.

'She wouldn't do that,' replied Hannah.

'She's probably helping Nana Ferndale with the washing. Don't forget she's been away for four weeks,' said Abi.

What Hannah and Abi didn't know was that Josh was deliberately keeping Rosie occupied so she didn't talk to her friends and when she did call the pub their father forgot to pass on her messages.

For the rest of the summer holiday they didn't get

to talk to each other although it was frequently discussed.

'I never liked her anyway,' lied Hannah.

'She only pretended to be our friend,' agreed Abi.

'I expect that she planned it,' said Abi stamping on the floor. 'If Mum dies it will be all her fault.'

'She's not pretty enough to be in our group anyway,' replied Hannah.

Life got cold

When the new term began Abi and Hannah were subdued and upset for their mother and secondly with the frustration of not being able to prove that they did write the song. They agreed that they would not mention what had happened to anyone and kept their distance from Rosie.

Rosie was unaware of Josh's success and because Abi and Hannah ignored her she reluctantly went her own way and made new friends who she spent all her spare time with.

Mrs Evans, their form teacher, noticed the change in Hannah and Abigail and the following lunchtime took them aside.

'I know your mother is very ill but it seems there is something else bothering the two of you. Can I help?' she asked in a soft understanding voice.

She was met with silence.

Hannah and Abi agreed to skip the dance group and the next afternoon Mrs Simpson stopped them as they were leaving school.

'I haven't seen you in my dance group since we came back to school. Is there a reason for that?' she asked.

The sisters said nothing.

Mrs Simpson continued. 'Knowing how much you love my classes I'm really surprised you aren't coming any more,' she said.

Abi was about to reply and Hannah, sensing it, nudged her in the ribs.

'Well if you do change your minds I would love to have you back,' said Mrs Simpson with a friendly smile. 'Please think about it girls.'

She patted them on the shoulders and walked

towards the staff room.

When she entered the staff room Mrs Evans was making a cup of tea.

'I don't know if it's me but have you noticed the change in Hannah and Abigail?' she asked.

Mrs Evans nodded. 'There is a problem but I can't put my finger on it,' she said as she sipped thoughtfully at her tea. 'I think I'll call Mr Thomas and see if he knows anything,' she said as she reached for the telephone.

The next morning Mrs Simpson addressed the whole school at assembly.

'We're not sure if you are aware but Hannah and Abigail's mother is very ill and we,' she hesitated and smiled at the teachers on the stage, 'the school… have decided we want to help. We have decided to help and raise some of the money for her to go to America for what is a very special treatment,' she explained. 'I have discussed the matter with Mr Thomas and we will be holding a fundraising karaoke afternoon in a marquee in the pub grounds of the Hare and Hounds to raise money for their mother to travel to America and get that treatment.'

The whole school clapped loudly as the shock on Hannah and Abi's faces turned to smiles of relief.

Rosie immediately rushed across to the sisters and tried desperately to talk to them but they ignored her.

The following day the bus ground to a halt as they made their way home. George tried desperately to get it to start but it groaned and smoked and then there was silence.

'I'm sorry girls but there's no way this bus is going anywhere. I'm going to suggest we all walk to the main road and wait for a replacement,' said George apologetically. 'Come on everybody leave your homework and we'll get on with it.'

The cheers were deafening as they all rushed off the bus.

"Take care girls,' shouted George. 'Walk in

single file.' He paused as the girls filled the narrow country lane. 'And… don't run!' he said.

As they all walked along the country lane Hannah could hold her silence no longer and she caught up with Rosie.

'How could you do it?' asked Hannah.

'Do what?' questioned Rosie.

'Come on, we know what you did,' shouted Abi.

'Yeah, just admit it!' screamed Hannah.

Rosie stopped abruptly and threw her blazer onto the dusty ground. 'I don't know what you're talking about,' she said.

'I suppose Josh paid for your pony?' shouted Abi.

'Josh? My pony? What are you talking about?' asked Rosie, trying not to get angry.

Abi found it hard to hold back her tears and in sheer desperation she broke down.

'Come on Rosie. You know we needed that money to take our mother to America. Now we've got no chance. You've ruined everything!' shouted Abi.

Hannah joined in. 'How could you keep quiet and let Josh take all the credit?' she said.

'But even worse you let him collect the prize money,' shouted Abi.

'Prize money… what prize money?' repeated Rosie, getting more confused every second.

'Seven thousand pounds,' answered Abi.

'Yeah, seven thousand pounds, that's how much it was,' added Hannah.

Rosie, now exhausted, sat down and leaned against a large oak tree, taking shelter from the warm afternoon sun.

'I don't know what it is. But I honestly haven't got a clue what you are both talking about,' pleaded Rosie.

Hannah spoke slowly and clearly. 'You remember our song?' she asked.

Rosie nodded in agreement and Hannah continued. 'Well somehow, Josh….'

'Your brother…,' interrupted Abi.

'Stole our song,' continued Hannah.

'How on earth did he do that?' asked Rosie rendered almost speechless.

'But... wait for it…,' interrupted Abi excitedly.

'Our song won the competition,' blurted out Hannah.

'But that's fantastic,' said Rosie with a wide smile.

'Sure it is,' sneered Abi.

'That's what we thought. But Josh said it was his song and he collected the seven thousand pounds that we needed it to take our mother to America,' continued Hannah.

'Josh? Surely there's some mistake. Why would Josh do that?' argued Rosie.

'We've got no idea?' asked Hannah.

'What we want to know is? What are you going to do about it?' shrieked Abi.

Rosie nodded her head. 'Well, that's a difficult one. We need to get Josh to admit that he didn't write the song and then I suppose you will get the money,' she said.

Rosie suddenly felt relieved at knowing the reason for the treatment that she had recently received from Abi and Hannah.

She smiled the widest smile. 'Leave it to me,' she said.

Caught in a moment

Josh, having raised the seven thousand pounds needed to go on his college trip to Africa, was busy making the final preparations. As always, he paid little attention to Rosie and she chose not to mention that she knew his secret.

While Rosie schemed, Abi and Hannah spent the time writing to the pop stars' fan clubs for their help. The response was disappointing, a few signed photographs, old CD's and a Tee shirt, followed by rejection, after rejection, after rejection.

Rosie finally had her chance when Josh went up

into the attic to collect his knapsack and walking boots. She climbed the ladder and bolted the loft hatch, removed the ladder and waited.

Within a few minutes Josh started to shout.

'Help… someone help me… unbolt the door!' he screamed. 'What sort of joke is this?'

Nana Ferndale didn't hear him and Rosie went to bed and covered her ears with her father's headphones.

Josh didn't sleep but became exhausted as he shouted, screamed and hammered on the loft floor, all the while getting more upset that he would miss his trip to Africa.

The next morning with only a few hours remaining before he was due to leave, Rosie shouted up to him from the landing.

'Is that you up there Josh?' she asked innocently.

'Come on Rosie, the doors bolted and I can't get down… can you help me or I'm going to miss the plane?' he shouted.

Rosie feigned ignorance. 'Pardon Josh… what did you say?'

'You heard… just unbolt the door… what is going on?' he screamed, his voice cracking with exhaustion.

Rosie now switched on her father's tape recorder and tapped the microphone gently. With the level indicator moving erratically she held the microphone nearer to the closed hatch.

'Josh… guess what?' she asked.

'What! What on earth is going on?' he asked, 'I haven't got time for this.'

'If I told you a silly story what would you think?' she asked.

'I'm not interested in stories…,' he fumed, 'Just get me out of here will yer,' he screamed.

Rosie repeated it again. 'Josh, if I told you a silly story what would you say?'

This time there was silence.

She switched on the tape recorder and climbed

the ladder to within a few inches of the closed hatch and held the microphone against the tiny gap.

'Josh, did you steal Hannah's and Abigail's song?' she asked.

'What?' replied Josh.

'You heard what I said.' She waited and then continued. 'If you want to catch your plane you ought to admit it.'

She heard movement above her and could hear him near the hatch. Suddenly he freaked out and screamed like a man possessed. 'Rosie! Open this door or… I'll kill you!'

Rosie remained silent and waited.

His voice suddenly changed. 'Come on Rosie… open the door. I didn't mean to shout like that. Come on, open up,' he pleaded.

Rosie now had a dilemma.

Should she let her brother out and let down her friends or help them as she had promised?

She slowly reached for the bolt but hesitated.

She remembered why she was doing this and how sick Hannah and Abigail's mother was and why they needed the money.

'No Josh, you tell me you stole Hannah and Abi's song and I'll open up,' she said.

Josh suddenly relented and blurted out.

'There's no way anyone will believe you. Just look at yourself, you're only ten,' he sniggered. 'Why should they believe you rather than me? Everyone will think that you've imagined it. Go on then, tell the World, who cares?' he threatened.

Rosie unbolted the hatch and Josh slid it open.

As Josh poked his head through the hatch Rosie pretended to cry, 'They will believe me, just you wait and see.'

Josh looked down at her from the ceiling hatch and gave her a dirty look.

'Try it, and see if I care anyway. Who do you think would believe that your baby friends would have been able to write a song as good as that?' he said mimicking her girlie voice.

Rosie checked the tape recorder was still recording, climbed down the ladder, pulled it away and waited. It didn't take more than a few minutes and Josh began to get angry.

'Can you get that ladder and put it back or I'm going to miss my plane? Come on Rosemary, let me down from here!' he screamed.

'Why did you do it Josh?' asked Rosie trying to trick her brother.

'Do what?' questioned Josh.

'Come on Josh, surely you're not going to lie to *me* are you?' asked Rosie.

'OK, I'll tell you what happened,' he said. 'After Abi and Hannah left our house I found the cassette and played it. It was good, and I knew that if I could win the radio songwriting competition, then I would have enough money to go to Africa with my mates from College,' said Josh.

'So you did steal their song?' asked Rosie.

'It was easy. I knew that they only had one

tape, so it wasn't a problem. It was simple… so simple,' answered Josh. 'Now will you put that ladder back, I swear I'm going to miss my plane.'

'How could you do such a thing Josh?' asked Rosie.

'I already told you why,' he shouted.

Before Rosie put the ladder back she replayed the cassette tape to Josh who became very angry.

Josh smiled down at her and once again mimicked her young friends. 'Anyway, what would they do with the money? Buy tons of sweets? They don't need it,' he said.

Josh looked at his watch and then started to shout at her. 'Come on let me down from here. Or, I'm going to miss my plane!' he demanded.

Rosie ignored his pleas and thought about the nasty things he had just said about her friends before answering. She then surprised him with her new found confidence and for a moment she sounded grown up.

'That's where you're wrong. Their mother is

very ill. She might even die,' she said.

'Who told you that?' he shouted. 'You've always been a sucker.'

Rosie looked up at him as he peered through the attic opening and she remembered the numerous times that he had treated her badly and teased her whenever she did anything that her mother and father complemented her on.

She now put the cassette in her jacket pocket and, after pushing the ladder against the attic opening, ran down the stairs and out of the front door, slamming it closed behind her.

The Promise

Josh slid down the metal ladder onto the wide landing, taking care to avoid knocking his mother's favourite vase. He picked up the telephone and phoned Jimmy, his best friend from College, and after hurriedly packing his haversack he ran downstairs.

Nana Ferndale, oblivious to the goings on, was busy in the kitchen preparing lunch. Josh pushed past her as he grabbed a handful of sliced bread and cheese before rushing to meet Jimmy who was walking up the drive.

Jimmy and Josh put their knapsacks in the boot

of his father's Mercedes saloon. Jimmy sat in the back while Josh joined his father in the front.

Already short of time Mr Ferndale noisily pulled away, throwing the loose gravel up into the air and across the manicured lawn and flowerbeds.

'Did you say goodbye to Rosemary?' asked his father as he drove down the narrow country lane.

'Yes, of course I did,' lied Josh.

As the car raced towards the M5 and Heathrow airport, Josh sat back, pleased that he had managed to get away with his deception, and that he would soon be on the plane jetting to Africa with Jimmy and the rest of the expedition.

After travelling for nearly an hour the car phone rang loudly, waking Josh from a doze. He looked down and noticed it was the telephone number of their house back in Littlehampstead. He thought very quickly and, pretending to sneeze, he reached down and cut off the call. It rang again almost immediately and he did exactly the same thing. This happened several times until the calls stopped coming and he returned to his state of semi consciousness.

Mr Ferndale drove them to the departure drop off point at the Heathrow terminal, unloaded their bulging misshapen haversacks from the boot of the Mercedes, and after a brief hug with Josh and a friendly handshake with Jimmy he drove off.

When he reached the motorway, Mr Ferndale slipped a blank CD into the player and listened to the latest demo recordings of a new group that he was keen to sign to his record label.

After two tracks, his car phone bleeped and a text message appeared on the screen:

Josh has stolen Abi and Hannah's song….
Please stop him before it's too late.
>   ***Rosie xx***

Mr Ferndale read it twice and then dialled his home number.

Nana Ferndale answered and after several

minutes he was able to make her understand that he wanted to talk to Rosemary.

'What's going on?' asked her father.

'He hasn't left has he?' pleaded Rosie.

'Rosie, who do you mean?' He found it hard to concentrate as he drove down the motorway.

'Come on what's happened? Why are you so upset?' He tried to calm Rosie down but she continued to cry hysterically.

'He... e… e… ddd... did it, it's all his fault,' sobbed Rosie.

'What are you talking about? Who did what?' he asked.

She couldn't speak fast enough and blurted out sentence after sentence until she ran out of breath. 'Yes. Josh… he stole a song that Abi and Hannah wrote for a radio competition, and now they won't be able to send their mother to America for an operation and she will die if we don't get the money.' She stopped to catch her breath and continued. 'He's not gone has he?'

'I don't want to disappoint you but, yes, Josh has gone. I expect he will have already boarded his plane.' He paused as he overtook a lorry. 'Now what's this all about?' he asked, 'Start again.'

Rosie took her time to tell her father what had happened. She explained how she had locked Josh in the attic and that she had tricked him into admitting that he had stolen the song and that she had the cassette of him admitting it.

'Alright, when I get home we'll talk about it. Now, ask Nana Ferndale to make you a nice cup of tea and I will be home in about an hour,' he said reassuringly.

Lush life

When her father arrived Rosie ran out to meet him. She sobbed in his arms, mumbling incoherent words and phrases. She sat in silence while she played the cassette to her father and as soon as it had finished he drove her to the Hare and Hounds, and explained to Abi and Hannah's father what had happened.

'I'm sorry. I can only apologise for Josh. He's not a bad lad but he thought that he was cleverer than the girls and now he will pay,' said Mr Ferndale.

He slowly sipped his beer. 'Look, you've got that marquee in the garden.'

'Ye... es,' replied Mr Thomas although he didn't understand what Rosie's father was getting at.

'Well Bob, if you've got that space, it will be ideal. Don't you think so?' he asked.

Abi and Hannah's father stood looking at Rosie's father getting more and more confused.

'What I mean is, why don't we arrange a charity gig for one afternoon next weekend?' asked Mr Ferndale.

'It sounds good to me, but how do you know that we will get anyone famous to come along?' asked Bob.

Rosie's father looked at him thinking all the time. 'Leave that to me,' he said. 'I thought that you knew I worked for a record company.'

'No, I had no idea,' answered Bob, preoccupied with serving his other customers.

During the next few days, Rosie's father arranged for his record company promotions team to contact the local radio, television stations and newspapers to promote the charity concert.

Abi, Hannah and Rosie rehearsed their dance routine with Mrs Simpson and, without telling the sisters, she secretly arranged for all the girls in the dance group to join in the finale.

Saturday morning came, the day of the concert. The weather was perfect, not too hot, with thin high wispy clouds and not a hint of rain.

The parents agreed that Hannah and Abi would be kept busy away from the pub and their father gave them errands to do in the village. When they returned home they were whisked to their bedroom by Rosie who helped them to get ready.

When they finally came downstairs the marquee was full to the brim and people were standing in the car park and pub gardens.

Television camera crews and their large satellite transmission vans filled the remainder of the pub car park, while newspaper photographers and reporters mixed with the crowd.

'I can't believe it,' said Abi to her sister.

'I thought dad might have rounded up a few people and the girls from school, but nothing like this,' said Hannah almost lost for words.

Rosie grabbed them and led them to the back of the stage. 'We're on in a few minutes,' she said excitedly.

They both looked at her.

'What do you mean, *we're* on in a few minutes?' asked Hannah.

Rosie was taken aback and she answered nervously. 'Well you did say all three of us could dance,' she said, her voice quivering with nerves.

'No, I didn't mean you dancing with us was a problem but I didn't know we were going to perform today,' said Hannah.

'I can't remember the dance let alone the words,' said Abi, looking very pale.

At that moment Rosie's father walked over to them. 'Are you ready then?' he asked.

'I don't think we can remember it,' said

Hannah, her voice shaking with nerves.

'Nor do I,' said Abi, her teeth chattering with fear.

'Once you get on stage you'll be fine… remember you are amongst friends.' He paused. 'And remember why we're doing this,' he said with a reassuring smile.

The girls looked at him blankly then smiled as they knew it was for their mother's treatment and suddenly their nerves were gone.

'Come on let's do it,' shouted Abi.

They heard their music, which sounded much better than their karaoke recording.

'We re-recorded it for you. After all, for such an important day, we had to do the best,' said Mr Ferndale.

He looked at the three of them and smiled.

'Isn't that right Rosie?' he said.

'All right… let's go,' shrieked Hannah and they ran onto the stage.

The crowd went crazy, screaming, shouting

and whistling, and before they knew it the girls had finished their song and didn't want to leave the stage.

Their euphoria was short lived as the intro of *'Push the button,'* boomed out and the Sugababes ran onto the stage to even louder screams.

Even Rosie was taken by surprise until her father winked slyly at her. She ran over and kissed him and gave him a huge hug.

'Thanks Dad, you're wonderful,' she shouted in his ear.

He bent down and whispered to her. 'Don't let Hannah and Abi go anywhere,' he said.

The Sugababes left the stage and as the intro of *'Sound of the Underground,'* blasted out, Cheryl and the other members of Girls Aloud raced on stage.

As soon as they finished the song the Sugababes joined them on stage and together they sang *'Walk This Way.'*

As the music faded and the crowd screamed

for more, Cheryl put her finger to her lips and suddenly there was silence.

'Thank you for coming,' she said. 'Have you enjoyed it?' she asked.

The crowd screamed and shrieked back at her. 'Ye e e as!!!!!!! Ye e eas!!!'

The cameras and mobile phones flashed and the television cameras moved across the stage filming every second.

Hannah, Abi and Rosie were so happy they cried.

'I can't believe it, how did they get to know about us,' said Hannah wiping her eyes.

'Yeah… I'm so pleased the girls from school are here because they would never believe me on Monday,' chipped in Abi.

Rosie smiled at them. 'My Dad asked them to come,' she said proudly.

'Your Dad? How come?' asked Hannah and Abi simultaneously.

'They're signed to his record label and when

he told them about you they jumped at the opportunity to help you and your Mum,' she said.

The crowd started to chant. 'Hannah… Abi… Hannah… Abi.'

Each time the chanting got louder and louder.

"They're calling you,' said Rosie. 'Go on they want you to go back on,' she said pushing them towards the stage.

Hannah and Abi were led towards the stage by Rosie's father and when they nervously walked on they were immediately hugged by their idols.

Cameras flashed and the brightly coloured stage lights spun around the white walls of the marquee, and television cameras continued to capture the moment.

Heidi Range now walked up to the microphone, put her arms around the three girls and waited until the hysteria subsided.

Then she spoke to the crowd.

'We hope you've all enjoyed today. We've had great fun and it's wonderful to see so many people turning up to help 'my friends.' On behalf of all of you and the girls I would like to present a cheque to Hannah and Abigail for fifteen thousand pounds,' she said.

Hannah mouthed the figure to Abi and Rosie.

'How much?' asked Abi.

'Heidi said fifteen thousand pounds,' replied Hannah proudly.

The radio DJ then walked on stage and took the microphone from Heidi and ushered Hannah and Abi to the front of the stage.

'I know that you both wrote the winning song back in the summer and I'm really sorry you didn't get the prize money. Unfortunately, we didn't know that until a few days ago but now we would like to make it up to you and I would like to present you with a cheque for seven thousand pounds,' he said.

He handed Abi the cheque and kissed her on the cheek. They stood and posed for even more photographs and shook with excitement.

'Oh… I nearly forgot,' he teased. 'There is one more thing…,' he paused again. 'I can tell everyone here today that the Sugababes and Girls Aloud will be recording your song, *'We're gonna be famous,'* for release later this year.'

Abi fainted with shock but was caught by Rosie while Hannah shook her head in total disbelief.

Mrs Evans and Mrs Simpson then joined them on stage followed by the rest of the dance group and presented them with a cheque for five hundred and forty pounds raised from a collection at the school.

The DJ took to the microphone once again.

'Would you like to hear Hannah and Abigail's song one more time?' he asked the audience.

The screams were close to unbearable as he tried to continue. 'And… and….'

He stood waving his arms and shaking his head in sheer disbelief until the screaming subsided.

'OK… would you like Girls Aloud and the Sugababes to sing it with them?' he screamed.

His question was totally unnecessary but drove the audience wild as they all moved nearer to the stage.

The music started and the girls from the school's dance group joined Abi, Hannah and Rosie on stage. When Hannah and Abi started to sing the second chorus Heidi, Keisha and Amelle joined Girls Aloud.

The television cameramen rushed around the stage filming from every angle as the girls sang their hearts out.

After the show Hannah, Abi and Rosie posed for photographs with their favourite singers and were given signed CD's, posters and T-shirts before the two groups left in stretch limousines.

Hannah, Abi and Rosie slept until Sunday lunchtime and by the time they were awake the marquee had gone and all that was left to prove it really happened was the outline of the marquee on the grass, and the souvenirs which were scattered around their bedroom.

Their father brought them breakfast in bed and sat on the end of Abi's bed while they ate their toast.

'That was one hell of a night, eh girls?' he said. 'I'm really proud of you and we have more than enough money to take your mother to America,' he said.

'I know,' said Abi, 'I added it up when I was on stage.'

Their father continued. 'It's fantastic. I've already spoken to Doctor Fitzsimmons and he is arranging for us to go over to America next week.' he said.

'Us?' asked Hannah. She looked across at Abi. 'All of us?' she questioned. 'Do you mean that? I mean we're all going?' She looked at Abi and wiped her eyes. 'We're all going to America?'

'Yes,' he paused. 'All of us,' said her father

with a wide smile.

'I've spoken to Mrs Simpson and she has already cleared it with the head teacher so we can all go. You deserve it ya know,' he said.

'Does Mum know yet?' asked Abi.

''Course she does. She was awake most of the night… she's only just gone to sleep. She was absolutely exhausted,' he said as he stood up. 'Oh, and I nearly forgot… she loved your song.'

He gave them a huge smile.

'We're gonna be famous are we girls?' he said.

Later that afternoon Mr and Mrs Ferndale drove Nana and Rosie over to the Hare and Hounds for a meal. Everyone was talking about the excitement of the previous day and the pub was busier than it had ever been.

When they arrived Bob called up to Hannah and Abi to tell them that Rosie and her family had arrived and the girls rushed down to meet them.

'Thank you so much for what you did, Mr

Ferndale,' said Hannah.

'Do you know Take That?' asked Abi.

Mr Ferndale laughed.

'No, but I do know Britney… and if you're good perhaps I can get some tickets for one of her shows when she comes over next year,' he said as he walked towards the bar.

He turned. 'Anyway, you're both celebrities now so you should be able to get your own tickets,' he said with a very loud laugh.

Mr Ferndale stood at the bar and smiled to himself while he waited to be served.

'Rushed off your feet I see today, Bob,' he said.

'Yeah, I should say so,' said Bob as he poured the drinks. 'I can't thank you enough for yesterday,' he said. 'Not only have we got enough to pay for Emily's treatment but we can all afford to go.'

'If you think about it, in a strange way it's all

down to Josh. He stole something that wasn't his and just look what happened,' said Mr Ferndale as he shook his head before continuing. 'He won't get away with it. No way will he,' he said firmly. 'And I'm going to make sure he repays the money… every last pound. Don't you worry about that.'

Bob carefully placed the drinks on a tray and looked across at the three girls as they spoke animatedly to each other and compared autographs.

'Thanks again… the drinks are on the house,' he said. 'I really don't think I can ever thank you enough.'

'It's nice to be able to help genuine people, especially so near to home,' he said.

As he walked towards the table Bob mouthed a final thank you to him.

Bonus track

The plane cut its way through the clouds and approached Heathrow airport. Emily Thomas smiled a contented smile as Hannah and Abi chattered excitedly to each other in their seats across the aisle.

'They've really grown up over the last few weeks, haven't they Bob?' she said.

'Yeah they have, and I'll never be able to thank them enough for what they've done,' he said as he wiped a tear from his eye and squeezed her hand.

'Now that you're getting better, Emily,' he

said, as he fought to choke his emotion. 'I'm going to sell the pub and get a job with regular hours so we can enjoy being a family.'

'That will be nice,' she said.

She nodded slowly.

'I'd like that Bobby,' she said, and looked out of the window to hide her tears of happiness.

'Now I know I'll be a star one day, Hannah,' said Abi as she smiled at her big sister.

'I believe you… so will I,' said Hannah as she grinned and nodded.

We're gonna be famous

www.ingramcontent.com/pod-product-compliance
Lightning Source LLC
Chambersburg PA
CBHW031320060726
47590CB00003B/1278